Dear Parent:

Your child's love of reading starts here.

Every child learns to read in a different way and at his or her own speed. Some go back and forth between reading levels and read favorite books again and again. Others read through each level in order. You can help your young reader improve and become more confident by encouraging his or her own interests and abilities. From books your child reads with you to the first books he or she reads alone, there are I Can Read Books for every stage of reading:

SHARED READING
Basic language, word repetition, and whimsical illustrations, ideal for sharing with your emergent reader

BEGINNING READING
Short sentences, familiar words, and simple concepts for children eager to read on their own

READING WITH HELP
Engaging stories, longer sentences, and language play for developing readers

READING ALONE
Complex plots, challenging vocabulary, and high-interest topics for the independent reader

I Can Read Books have introduced children to the joy of reading since 1957. Featuring award-winning authors and illustrators and a fabulous cast of beloved characters, I Can Read Books set the standard for beginning readers.

A lifetime of discovery begins with the magical words "I Can Read!"

Visit www.icanread.com for information on enriching your child's reading experience.

Clarion Books is an imprint of HarperCollins Publishers.
I Can Read® and I Can Read Book® are trademarks of HarperCollins Publishers.

Big Dog and Little Dog Going for a Walk
Copyright © 1997 by Dav Pilkey
All rights reserved. Printed in the United States of America. No part of this book may be used or reproduced in any manner whatsoever without written permission except in the case of brief quotations embodied in critical articles and reviews. For information address HarperCollins Children's Books, a division of HarperCollins Publishers, 195 Broadway, New York, NY 10007.
www.icanread.com

Library of Congress Control Number: 2023947886
ISBN 978-0-06-337351-8 (trade bdg.) — ISBN 978-0-06-337350-1 (pbk.)

Typography by Jon Corby
24 25 26 27 28   LB   10 9 8 7 6 5 4 3 2 1

First I Can Read edition, 2024

Big Dog and Little Dog
Going for a Walk

Dav Pilkey

CLARION BOOKS
An Imprint of HarperCollinsPublishers

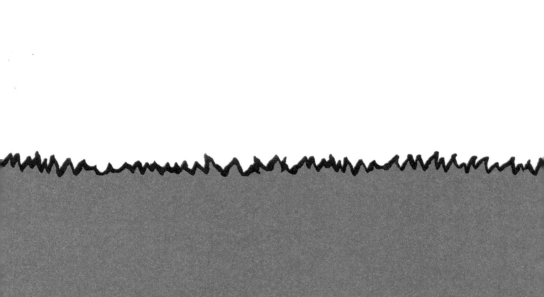

To Nathan Douglas Libertowski

Big Dog is going for a walk.

Little Dog is going, too.

Little Dog likes to play
in the mud.

Big Dog likes to eat the mud.

Little Dog likes to splash
in the puddles.

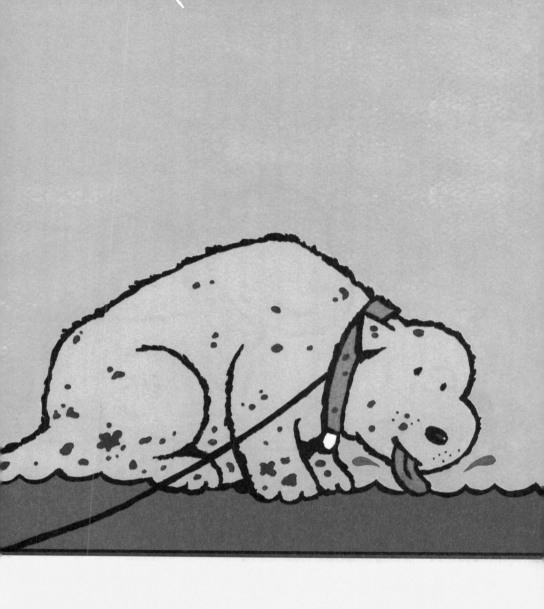

Big Dog likes to drink
the puddles.

Big Dog and Little Dog
had a fun walk.

They are very dirty.

It is time to take a bath.

Big Dog and Little Dog
are in the tub.

Now it is time to dry off.

Big Dog and Little Dog
shake and shake.

Big Dog and Little Dog
are clean and dry.

Now they want to go for
another walk.

🐾 Only Opposites 🐾

**"Big" and "little" are opposites.
Can you match more opposites
in the word list below?**

🐾 dirty   🐾 dry

🐾 wet   🐾 go

🐾 stop   🐾 slow

🐾 fast   🐾 clean

🐾 Picture It 🐾

**Read the sentences below.
Can you match them
with the correct image?**

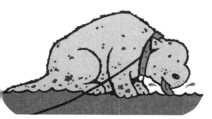

Big Dog and Little Dog
are in the tub.

Little Dog likes to play
in the mud.

Big Dog likes to drink
the puddles.

Big Dog and Little Dog
are going for a walk.

:paw: Story Sequencing :paw:

The story of Big Dog and Little Dog
going for a walk got scrambled!
Can you put the scenes in the right order?

A

B

C

D

E